NORMAN BRIDWELL

Clifford
GROWS UP

Hi! I'm Emily Elizabeth and
I want to show you some special
pictures of my dog Clifford.
You'll notice that he has grown up a lot!

When Clifford was a puppy,
he was so tiny that I had to
feed him with my doll's bottle.

And he was so small that I could
dress him up in my doll's clothes.

And he liked to hide in my dollhouse.

Even the smallest collar I could
find was too big for him.

And when he began to eat dog food,
I had to watch him all the time.

My puppy's first snow day
was a big adventure.

Here is a picture of a snowman I made with my friend.

I wanted Clifford to be in the picture, too.

Do you know what?

He was!

Here I was making valentines.

Clifford made one, too!

When summer came, Clifford chased birds.
But he never caught one.

In autumn, Clifford chased falling leaves.
He had fun!

In this picture, Clifford was playing football.

Clifford even scored a touchdown!

On Halloween, Clifford liked
the Jack-o'-lantern.

Clifford was the littlest ghost
I had ever seen.

That Halloween, Clifford discovered candy apples.

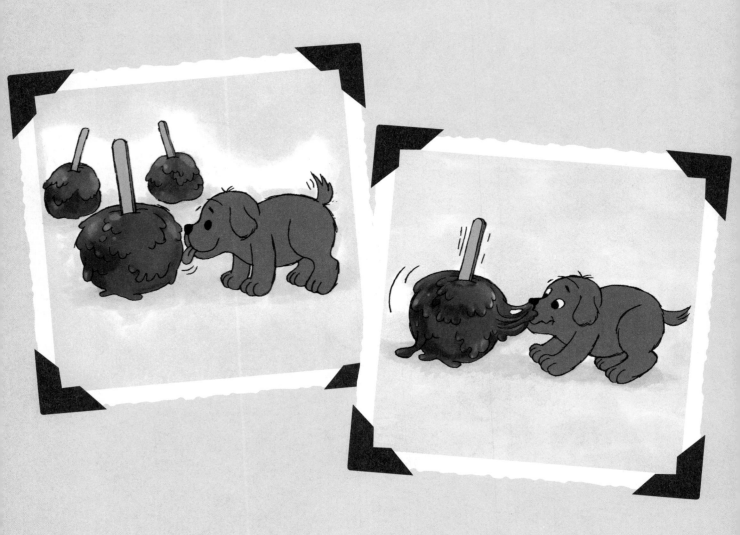

The candy was sort of sticky!

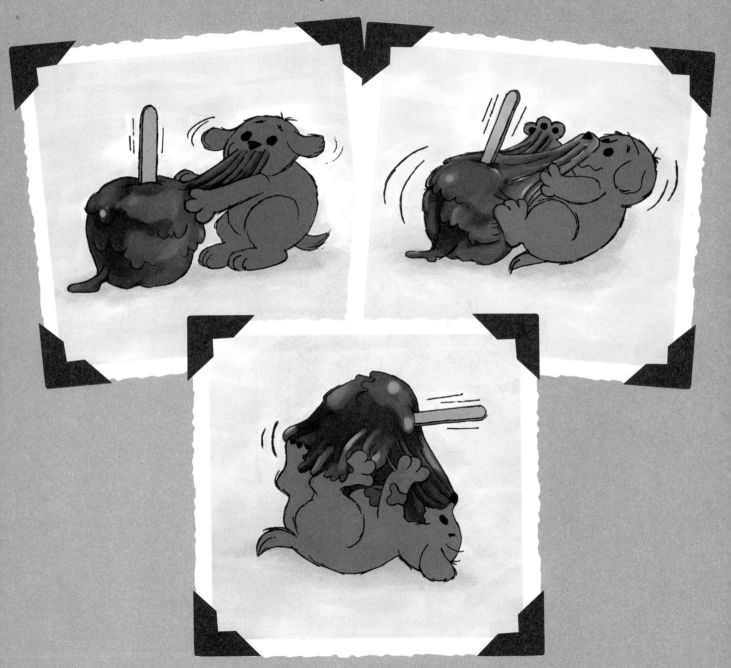

Before Christmas, Clifford helped
me wrap presents.

Clifford's first present from Santa was a bone.

For the new year, we had a wonderful surprise.
Clifford began to grow.

He grew some more.

And he grew some more.

We had to move from the city to the country.
This picture shows Clifford on moving day.

And this is Clifford all grown up.

I love my big red dog!

NORMAN BRIDWELL

Oops, Clifford!®

Hi! I'm Emily Elizabeth.
I have the biggest, reddest dog on our street.

This is my dog — Clifford.

Oh, I know he's not perfect.
He makes mistakes sometimes.

One day, Clifford and I were doing good deeds with our friend Tim. Somebody had let the air out of the tires of a car. The man asked if we could help him.

Tim took a rubber tube out of the car and stuck it on the tire valve. Then he told Clifford to blow air through the tube.

The man felt better
when we took his car to a garage.

Clifford also did a good deed when the circus came to town. The owner said everything was going wrong. He didn't think they could put on the show.

I told him Clifford and I would help him. He didn't think a girl and her dog could be much help. But I said, "The show must go on."

Clifford put on a clown costume and joined the act. Clifford enjoyed being a clown.

He wagged his tail. Oops!
That made the act even better.

One day, two nice police officers asked me about my dog.
I told them he could do tricks.

Then I told Clifford to roll over.

Oops! That was a mistake.

Later that day I saw a girl do a foolish thing. She was walking on the railing of a bridge.

Then she slipped.

Hooray for Clifford! He saved the girl.

The policemen were so happy that they forgave Clifford for mashing their car.

Clifford may not be perfect . . . but I love him just the same!